The Black Dog Who Went Into The Woods

The Black Dog Who Went Into The Woods

by Edith Thacher Hurd

Pictures by Emily Arnold McCully

HARPER & ROW, PUBLISHERS

To
Rosie and Ben

Library of Congress Cataloging in Publication Data
Hurd, Edith Thacher, date
    The black dog who went into the woods.

    SUMMARY: The various members of a family react to the
death of their dog.
    1. Dogs—Legends and stories. [1. Dogs—Fiction.
2. Death—Fiction] I. McCully, Emily Arnold.
II. Title.
PZ10.3.H964B1 1980   [E]   79-2000
ISBN 0-06-022683-8
ISBN 0-06-022684-6 lib. bdg.

"Black Dog has gone into the woods and died,"
Benjamin, the youngest one, said.

"Don't say such things," Rose, the middle one, said.

"Hey, Benj," Sammy, the oldest one, said. "What are you talking like that for?"

But Mother asked, "What are you saying, Youngest One?"

"I'm saying," the youngest one answered, "that Black Dog isn't here anymore. I've been looking all day for Black Dog, and she isn't anywhere."

"That doesn't mean she's dead," Rose, the middle one, said crossly.

"She'll come back," said Sammy.

"No, she won't," Benjamin said. "Black Dog is gone forever."

"Oh, I don't think so," Father said. "I'll go into the woods with you, Benj, and we will find her."

"I'll go," Benjamin said, "but we won't find her. Black Dog doesn't want us to find her."

So Mother and Father and Sammy, the oldest one, and Rose, the middle one, and Benjamin, the youngest one, all walked over the pasture, through the meadow and into the woods. It was summer, and the leaves were thick and green. The sun came through the leaves in little blots of golden light.

It was hot and nothing moved in the woods; just one small brown chipmunk scurried under a pile of old twigs. Benjamin remembered how Black Dog had liked to scare chipmunks.

All afternoon Mother and Father and Sammy and Rose and Benjamin walked and walked, looking in different places.

They called, "Here, Black Dog! Here, Black Dog!"

But they all knew that Black Dog was deaf. She hadn't been able to hear for a long time.

Benjamin was tired.

"I don't think we should look for Black Dog anymore," he said. "Black Dog doesn't want us to look for her."

"Perhaps Benjamin is right," Mother said.

So they all went home and nobody talked very much.

The summer evening was warm. In the deep sky there were yellow stars.

After supper Sammy went out several times and walked about in the night, but nobody asked what he had been doing when he came back into the house. The next day and for many days after that, Black Dog did not come home.

Sammy and Rose went to the brook where Black Dog

drank when she was thirsty. Sammy went to the old spring where Black Dog had fallen in when she was a puppy. She would not have gotten out if Sammy had not found her. But Benjamin, the youngest one, never went with them.

Mother called all the neighboring farmers, but nobody had seen Black Dog.

Then at last Rose said, "Benjamin may be right, Sammy. Black Dog was very old. Her legs were stiff. Do you think they hurt her?"

Sammy didn't know.

"If she had been able to bark, she would have barked to tell us where she was," he said.

"Only the youngest one could still talk to her," Rose said.

"Yes," Sammy answered, "they knew what they were saying to each other, Black Dog and Benj."

"I think," Father said, "that Benjamin understands better than any of us. Animals sometimes do go into the woods, or someplace, by themselves when they know it is time for them to die. Even elephants do this."

"I'm glad she is in our woods," Sammy said.

"We will always know she is there," Mother said.

That night the stars did not shine as brightly as usual, because over the pine trees a moon rose, yellow, fat and round. It was a full moon that night.

The moonlight slipped, inch by inch, into the big bedroom where Mother and Father were sleeping. It shone on Mother's face.

Mother's Dream

Mother is holding a ball of soft, warm, black fur. A tiny puppy is curled up, asleep in her arms. Mother and Father are bringing her home from a friend's house. She is the smallest puppy of the litter. Mother puts the little dog into Sammy's sleeping bag where he is sleeping on the sleeping porch. Sammy does not even know she is there.

Mother woke up. "Thank you, Black Dog," she whispered. "Thank you for coming to say good-bye to me." Then Mother was asleep again.

The moon touched Father's face, and he dreamed a dream in the moonlight.

Father's Dream

Father is lying in bed. He is listening. Is that Black Dog barking? Father gets out of bed. He shivers as he goes to the window.

Hard, icy snow covers the ground. A doe and her two fawns stand under a bare maple tree. Their ears point forward. They are listening. The deer stand as still as the bare tree, but Black Dog has heard their sharp hooves breaking the crust of the frozen snow. She has smelled their scent on the winter wind.

Black Dog barks over and over.

The doe leaps forward. Her two fawns follow her until they are only three black shadows moving across the shimmering whiteness.

"I'm glad she can't get out," Father says. "Black Dog must not chase the deer."

Father opened his eyes and pulled the covers around him.

"Your legs had grown too stiff to chase deer," he said. "You couldn't even have heard them. You couldn't even have barked at them anymore. Good-bye, old Black Dog."

In his own private room at the top of the house, the moonlight touched only the end of Sammy's bed, but somehow he knew it was there and Sammy dreamed a dream about Black Dog.

Sammy's Dream

A new spring sun shines through bare trees. Sammy and Black Dog are going around in the woods together. Black Dog is running and sniffing and scratching big holes in the soft ground. She is looking for chipmunks and mice.

"*You'll never find 'em.*" *Sammy laughs.*

Sammy and Black Dog run through the woods, zigzagging, jumping over rocks, over trees blown down by winter storms.

Sammy slips. His foot catches under a log. He falls. His head hits a rock. Sammy lies still.

Black Dog is far away in the woods, barking and hunting.

But suddenly she is there beside Sammy. Black Dog sniffs Sammy. She licks his face. They sit quietly until Sammy feels better. He gets up and he and Black Dog walk home together.

Now the moon shone on Sammy's face, and he woke up.

He touched his cheek but it was not wet from Black Dog's tongue, and Sammy knew that he had been dreaming.

"Thank you, Black Dog," Sammy said. "Thank you for coming back for me in the woods."

Then Sammy fell asleep again.

Rose was asleep but still she knew that the moonlight was touching her. It crept over her bed and a dream came to her.

Rose's Dream

It is summer and hot. Rose and Black Dog are swimming in the deep pool of the river. Black Dog swims with her strong back legs and her front paws going like paddle wheels. Her tail moves back and forth. She holds her black head high out of the water.

Rose swims beside Black Dog in the clear, cold river, and she hears Black Dog breathing hard as she swims.

"You puff like a steam engine," Rose says.

Then Rose gets out of the pool and dries herself with her towel. Black Dog scrambles out of the river and stands very close to Rose. She shakes water all over Rose and all over her dry clothes.

"Oh, Black Dog!" Rose yells. "You're a bad dog. Go away, Black Dog."

Rose turned over in bed. She opened her eyes and closed them again because the moonlight was too bright for her.

"Good-bye, Black Dog," she said softly. "I'm sorry I was cross with you."

Benjamin was asleep on the porch where Mother had first put little Black Dog into Sammy's sleeping bag.

Benjamin liked having the porch all for himself. He liked to go to sleep with the sound of the wind and the rain. He liked to wake up and listen for the early-morning thrushes singing in the woods and the crows calling from across the meadow.

Benjamin was asleep and he was dreaming.

Benjamin's Dream

Black Dog is sleeping on the floor beside Benjamin. Benjamin looks at Black Dog's legs and feet as they twitch and jump. Black Dog makes little squeaking noises and tiny barking sounds as she sleeps. She is dreaming.

"You think you're hunting, don't you?" Benjamin says. "But you're only dreaming, old dog."

Then it is morning and something is poking and pushing at Benjamin. He opens his eyes. Black Dog has her paws on his bed. A dirty sock hangs out of her mouth. She is snuffling and sniffing at Benjamin. He pulls on the old sock, but Black Dog will not let go. Benjamin pulls and pulls until he pulls Black Dog into bed with him. Then he covers her with his blankets so that Mother won't know that Black Dog is there.

The moonlight was so bright that Benjamin opened his eyes.

He felt with his hands, but Black Dog wasn't there under the covers beside him. Black Dog wasn't on the rug where she had always slept as long as Benjamin could remember.

"Thank you, Black Dog," he said. "Thank you for coming to say good-bye to me."

Then before the youngest one even knew it, he was asleep again.

Everyone was quiet at breakfast the next morning.

Only Benjamin said, "Black Dog came in the night to say good-bye to me."

"She came to me, too," said Mother.

Father nodded his head, and Sammy and Rose said, "She came to me." "And me, too."

"But mostly," Sammy said, "I think she came to say good-bye to Benjamin, because he could still talk to her."

Benjamin did not say anything more about Black Dog after that.